Jessica the matchmaker . . .

"Flowers," said the TV announcer. "They say all the things you'd like to say—but can't."

"Maybe Molly should buy some flowers," Elizabeth said. "They could tell Jack she was sorry."

I knew that was silly. Flowers can't talk. But it gave me an idea. Molly wouldn't say she was sorry. Jack wouldn't say he was sorry. But *I* would.

"I have a great idea!" I said.

"What is it?" Elizabeth asked.

"Do you want Molly and Jack to get back together?"

"Sure," Elizabeth said.

"Well, I know how to do it!" I told her.

Bantam Books in the SWEET VALLEY KIDS series

SWEET VALLEY KIDS

JESSICA PLAYS CUPID

Written by
Molly Mia Stewart

Created by
FRANCINE PASCAL

Illustrated by
Ying-Hwa Hu

BANTAM BOOKS
NEW YORK · TORONTO · LONDON · SYDNEY · AUCKLAND

RL 2, 005-008

JESSICA PLAYS CUPID
A Bantam Book / February 1995

*Sweet Valley High® and Sweet Valley Kids are
trademarks of Francine Pascal*

Conceived by Francine Pascal

*Produced by Daniel Weiss Associates, Inc.
33 West 17th Street
New York, NY 10011*

Cover art by Susan Tang

ISBN: 0-553-48207-6

Published simultaneously in the United States and Canada

Bantam Books are published by Bantam Books, a division of Bantam
Doubleday Dell Publishing Group, Inc. Its trademark, consisting of the
words "Bantam Books" and the portrayal of a rooster, is registered in the
U.S. Patent and Trademark Office and in other countries.   Marca
Registrada. Bantam Books, 1540 Broadway, New York, New York 10036.

PRINTED IN THE UNITED STATES OF AMERICA

0 9 8 7 6 5 4 3 2

To Gabriella Nardi

CHAPTER 1

Winston Shows Off

Hi! My name is Jessica Wakefield. I am seven years old.

I have a twin sister named Elizabeth. We are identical twins. That means she looks just like me.

I have blue-green eyes. Elizabeth does, too. Elizabeth has long blond hair with bangs, just like mine.

I love clothes. Elizabeth and I have a bunch that match. When we dress the same way, nobody can tell us apart! Sometimes we can even fool Mom and Dad and Steven.

Steven's our brother. He thinks he's great just because he's two years older than me and Elizabeth. But he's just a pain, like all the other boys I know.

Elizabeth and I are in second grade at Sweet Valley Elementary School. Our teacher is Mrs. Otis—she's the best! I sit right next to Elizabeth in class.

My favorite parts of school are recess and lunch and seeing my friends. Elizabeth loves *everything* about school—even the boring parts. Even homework! Elizabeth always does hers without being told. I hardly ever do.

My favorite friends at school are Lila Fowler and Ellen Riteman. They like to play with dolls and wear pretty clothes, just like I do. Lila thinks Elizabeth is a goody-goody. Sometimes Ellen and Lila make fun of Elizabeth.

I always try to make them stop.

Elizabeth's favorite school friends are Amy Sutton and Todd Wilkins. Amy and Elizabeth ride horses together. I think horses are smelly. Todd and Elizabeth are on the same soccer team. Elizabeth never misses a game. Not even when the field is muddy. Yuck!

Elizabeth acts like a tomboy sometimes. Not me! On the playground, I like to jump rope, play hopscotch, or swing on the swings. I'm the best jump-roper in my entire class. I also like to play the piano. I'm going to be an actress or a singer when I grow up. I'll have millions of adoring fans. Maybe I'll marry a prince and become a real-life princess.

A lot of people are surprised that Elizabeth and I are so different. They think we should be the same on the *inside* because we look the same on the *outside*. That's silly. No one else in the world is just like me. Mom and Dad say that even though I look like Elizabeth, I'm one of a kind!

Elizabeth and I are best friends. We are going to be best friends *forever.* I love being a twin, and so does she.

Do you know what else we love? Valentine's Day! Elizabeth and I love making valentines. We love getting them, too. And we really love eating candy hearts!

But we do not love the mushy part of Valentine's Day. That kissy-kissy stuff makes me sick. I, Jessica Wakefield, do not like boys. They run around on the playground and get sweaty and dirty. They open their mouths when they're eating so that you see the chewed-up food inside. If a boy ever tries to kiss me, I'll pinch him.

But lots of people disagree with me. They like the mushy part of Valentine's Day. *And* boys. Molly sure did. . . .

I held up the valentine I had just finished. "This one is for Mrs. Otis," I announced.

"It's pretty," Elizabeth said.

"Thanks," I answered happily.

It was a week before Valentine's Day. Elizabeth and I were sitting at an art table in our classroom. Six kids from our class—Lila, Ellen, Todd, Amy, Winston Egbert, and Kisho Murasaki— were sitting with us. We were all making valentines. The table was covered with red, pink, and white construction paper. There were also glue, glitter, and Magic Markers.

Winston was sitting at the other end of the table. He was making a lot of noise. Winston can be pretty funny sometimes, but I was getting tired of listening to him.

"Who should I make a card for now?" I asked Elizabeth.

Elizabeth thought for a second. "How about making one for Molly?" Molly was our new baby-sitter.

I frowned. "But we haven't even met her yet."

"We'll meet her this afternoon," Elizabeth pointed out.

I groaned. "I know."

"What's the matter?" Elizabeth asked.

"I don't like baby-sitters," I said. "I wish we could stay by ourselves, like Ellen does."

"Mom and Dad say we're too young," Elizabeth said.

"I know," I said again.

Our mother studies interior design. That means she's learning how to make rooms look pretty.

Mom had just gotten a big job. She was decorating an entire restaurant. The job had to be finished fast, so Mom had to work every afternoon. And we had to have a baby-sitter.

We hardly ever have baby-sitters. Once Mom and Dad went away on a trip together. We couldn't go because it was business. Great-Aunt Helen came to stay with us. We had fun. But that was different. Great-Aunt Helen isn't a *real* baby-sitter. She's a relative.

I was nervous about Molly. She might not make us snacks or let us go outside to play. Maybe she was one of those people who think TV is bad for you.

"I'm not making Molly a card until I meet her," I decided.

"OK," Elizabeth said. She was coloring. The tip of her tongue stuck out of her mouth.

"Eight!" Kisho announced proudly.

"I've already finished eight cards."

Winston laughed. "I haven't even finished one."

"That's because all you do is talk," I told him.

"I'm talking a lot because I'm excited," Winston explained.

"What are you excited about?" Amy asked.

"I just started taking juggling lessons," Winston said. "They're really fun."

Lila rolled her eyes. "There's no way you can juggle."

"Can so!" Winston jumped out of his seat. "I'll prove it. What do you want me to juggle?"

"I *don't* want you to juggle," Lila said.

But Todd looked around the table. "How about paste pots?"

"That's too hard," Ellen said. "Paste pots are heavy."

"I can do it," Winston said. "I'll use empty ones."

Winston walked around the classroom. He collected three paste pots. He threw them into the air one at a time. When the first one came down, he caught it. He caught the second one, too. But Winston missed the third one—it hit the floor right next to my foot. The lid fell off and bounced across the room. Paste splattered my favorite pink sneakers.

"Winston!" I yelled. "Look what you did."

"Oops," Winston said. "I'm sorry. I guess that one wasn't empty."

"You're a terrible juggler," I said.

"Winston said he was sorry," Elizabeth pointed out.

I didn't care that Winston was sorry. I was mad because of my sneakers.

"I knew you couldn't juggle," Lila told Winston.

"Well, I'm just learning," Winston said. "Juggling is hard. My teacher says beginners always drop things."

"It can't be *that* hard," I said.

"You don't know what you're talking about," Winston told me. "I bet you've never even tried to juggle."

"I haven't," I said. "But I can still juggle better than you can."

"Can not!" Winston shot back.

"Try it," Todd suggested.

I got up and took two paste pots from Winston. I picked the other one up off the floor and screwed its lid back on.

Everyone was watching me. I smiled. I love having an audience. I threw the first pot into the air. But I threw it too high. It fell faster than I expected. I couldn't catch it on the way down.

Everyone laughed.

"Winston is much better," Todd said.

The rest of the kids nodded. Even Lila.

"My fingers were slippery," I protested.

Everyone laughed some more.

"Besides," I added quickly, "it wasn't a fair contest. Winston has been practicing. He's been taking juggling lessons for a whole week!"

"That's true," Winston said. "But I dare you to a fair juggling contest. We'll have it seven days from now. I won't practice my juggling until then. That way you can catch up."

"Deal," I said.

CHAPTER 2

Wanted: Juggling Teacher

"Can I have your orange?" I asked Elizabeth at lunch.

Elizabeth gave me a funny look. "Why do you want my orange?" she asked. "You didn't eat yours yet."

"I'm not going to eat it," I explained. "I'm going to juggle it."

Elizabeth smiled and handed me her orange.

"I need one more thing," I said.

Eva Simpson gave me an apple.

"Thanks," I said. I tried to juggle the three pieces of fruit. I dropped the apple so many times that it got mushy.

"Yuck," Eva said when I handed it back to her.

"Sorry," I said with a giggle. "Here, you can have my orange. It's still OK."

On the playground, I tried to juggle rocks. But they were too heavy.

By the time we lined up to go inside, I was feeling grumpy. "I've been practicing my juggling all day," I told Elizabeth. "But I'm not getting any better."

"Maybe juggling is harder than you thought," Elizabeth said.

"Maybe." I sighed. "But how am I going to beat Winston?"

"You could get someone to teach you how to juggle," Elizabeth said.

I smiled. "Right! I need a teacher."

As soon as we got inside, I ran up to the teacher's desk. "Mrs. Otis?" I said. "Will you teach me to juggle?"

"I would," Mrs. Otis said. "But I don't know how to juggle. Maybe you can teach *me* after you learn."

I walked to my seat, disappointed. Who could be my juggling teacher? Elizabeth didn't know how to juggle. Neither did any of my friends. The only person I knew who could juggle was Winston. And he wasn't going to teach me.

We had gym that afternoon. Mr. Butler is our gym teacher. He always wears a whistle on a string around his neck. Mr. Butler knows the rules to lots of games. He's good at dodge ball.

I raised my hand as soon as my class had settled into a circle.

"Yes, Jessica?" Mr. Butler said.

"Will you teach me how to juggle?" I asked.

"Sorry," Mr. Butler said. "I don't know how to juggle."

15

Winston smirked at me.

I stuck my tongue out at him. I would show him. *I've got to find a juggling teacher,* I thought.

"Steven?" I said as we got on the bus after school. "Do you know how to juggle?"

"No," Steven said. He went to sit next to his friend Joe. Joe punched Steven in the arm. Then they started to wrestle.

I sat down next to Elizabeth and sighed. "Nobody I know can teach me how to juggle."

"Don't give up," Elizabeth said.

"I already asked about a million people and they all said no," I replied. "It's time to give up."

"Too bad," Elizabeth said. "Winston will win the juggling contest now."

I frowned. "Maybe Mom knows how to juggle."

"Maybe," Elizabeth said.

"I'm going to ask her as soon as we get home," I announced.

When the bus got to our stop, I jumped off before everyone else. Elizabeth was right behind me. We were way ahead of Steven.

"Let's run!" I yelled to Elizabeth.

Elizabeth and I raced home. I pushed open our front door and ran inside.

"Mom!" I yelled. "Where are you?"

There was no answer. That's when I remembered—Mom wasn't home. Molly, the new baby-sitter, was starting that afternoon. I had forgotten all about her.

Molly came out into the hallway. She had shoulder-length brown hair. "Hi!" she said. "You must be the twins. I'm Molly."

"I'm Elizabeth," my sister said.

"Hi," I added. "My name is Jessica."

I looked Molly over. Guess what—she was wearing pink sneakers. They were just like mine, except they were a little bigger. And they didn't have paste splattered on them. I was about to tell Molly how much I liked them when the door opened. Steven came in.

"Hi. I'm Molly."

"Hi," Steven said angrily. He was mad that we had a baby-sitter. He thinks he's too old for them.

"Your mother told me you guys would be hungry when you got home," Molly said. "How about a snack?"

"We'll eat later," Steven said quickly. "We have to do something in my room now. All three of us."

Molly gave Steven a puzzled smile. "Can I come, too?"

"No," Steven said. "It's a secret. Wakefields only."

Molly thought about that. "OK," she finally said. "When you guys get hungry, I'll be in the kitchen."

"Come on," Steven said to me and Elizabeth. He started up the stairs. Elizabeth and I followed.

"What's going on?" I whispered to Elizabeth.

Elizabeth shrugged. "Beats me."

I was curious. Steven doesn't let us into his room—he even has a sign on the door that says NO GIRLS ALLOWED. And he never *invites* us in. What was the secret?

When we got upstairs, Steven closed his door behind us. "I have plans for the new baby-sitter," he announced.

"What kind of plans?" Elizabeth asked.

"Plans to make her life miserable," Steven explained.

I bit my lip. Molly seemed pretty nice. Anyone who wore pink sneakers had to be cool. But I love to play tricks. Steven is good at thinking of them. And he had never offered to let me and Elizabeth help him before.

"What are we going to do?" I asked.

Elizabeth frowned. "Come on, you guys. Molly seems nice. Why do you want to play jokes on her?"

"Because she's the baby-sitter," Steven said.

"Right!" I put in.

"I don't know. . . ." Elizabeth said.

"If you don't want to help, that's fine," Steven told Elizabeth. "Jessica and I can do it without you. But I'll have to ask you to leave now. We have plans to make."

Steven walked over to the door and opened it. He motioned for Elizabeth to get out.

"No," Elizabeth said. "I don't want to leave. Tell me the plans, too."

Elizabeth doesn't like to play tricks. But she doesn't like to be left out, either.

CHAPTER 3

Funny Jokes

About twenty minutes later, Elizabeth, Steven, and I went downstairs together. My stomach was rumbling. I was very hungry.

We found Molly sitting at the kitchen table. She was reading a book for school.

"We're ready for our snack now," I announced.

"Great," Molly said. She got up and started toward the refrigerator. "Hey," she said as she passed me, "great sneakers."

"Thanks," I said. "I like yours, too."

Steven frowned at me. I stopped smiling. Oops! I had forgotten we were supposed to be mean to Molly.

Molly pulled out the bread, peanut butter, and jelly. She started to make sandwiches. When she finished the first one, Steven grabbed it. He took a big bite. Then he spat it out on the table.

"Eww," Elizabeth said.

"What is *this?*" Steven asked, tossing the sandwich down.

"A PBJ," Molly said.

"We can't eat PBJs," Steven said. "We always have cake for a snack."

"Always?" Molly asked, her eyes wide.

"Well, sometimes we have pie," Steven said.

Elizabeth and I managed to nod without laughing. Elizabeth smiled a little bit. But I didn't.

"Cake or pie every day?" Molly said. "How boring. You must be ready for a change." She went back to making sandwiches.

Steven frowned at his sandwich. Then he picked it up and took a big bite. This time, he swallowed.

Upstairs, Steven had told us Molly would definitely give us cake. That trick hadn't worked. But we still had one more to try.

"Here's your sandwich, Jessica," Molly said to me. She handed me a plate.

"Thanks," I said. "But I'm Elizabeth."

"Oops," Molly said. "I guess it will take me a while to get you two straight."

Elizabeth and I usually wear bracelets with our names on them. They help people tell us apart. But we had taken the bracelets off and left them in our room.

I took a bite of my sandwich.

Molly handed Elizabeth a plate. "Here you go, Jessica."

"Thanks," Elizabeth said.

Molly turned to me. "So, does everyone call you Elizabeth? Or do you like Liz, or Beth?"

I shrugged. "You can call me whatever you want. I don't care."

"That's not true!" Elizabeth exclaimed. "I—um, I mean, *she* likes to be called Elizabeth."

Molly nodded slowly. She looked right at me. "What do you like to be called, Jessica?"

I didn't answer.

Neither did Elizabeth.

I cleared my throat and glanced at Elizabeth. She still didn't say anything.

"Well, *Jessica?*" Steven asked. He gave Elizabeth a shove.

"Oh!" Elizabeth exclaimed. "You can just call me Jessica."

The corners of Molly's mouth twitched. She got up and walked over to the telephone.

Steven and Elizabeth and I traded looks. What was Molly doing?

Molly ripped two pieces of paper off the pad my mother keeps next to the phone. She wrote something on each piece. She also picked up a roll of tape. Molly came back to the table. She set everything down.

I leaned over and looked at the pieces of paper. One said ELIZABETH. The other said JESSICA.

"What are those?" I asked.

"Name tags," Molly said. "I want you to wear them."

"I don't want to," I complained.

"I'll make you a deal," Molly said. "If I can put the right name tag on the

right twin, you guys have to wear them."

"Deal," I said right away. Elizabeth and I had been pretending to be each other. Molly would never get the tags right.

"OK," Elizabeth agreed.

Molly put the JESSICA tag on me and the ELIZABETH tag on Elizabeth.

Elizabeth's jaw dropped. "How did you know?"

Molly winked at her. "I used to play tricks on my baby-sitters, too."

"What kind of tricks?" Steven asked.

"I'm not going to tell you," Molly said. "That would be crazy."

Steven started to laugh. Then he stopped suddenly. He turned red.

"Hey, Molly," I said. "Do you know how to juggle?"

Steven kicked my foot. He didn't want me to be nice to Molly, but I was getting tired of trying to trick her. She was too smart.

"No, I don't," Molly said. "But I have a friend who's a great juggler."

"Can we call her?" I asked.

"Him," Molly corrected me. "My friend's name is Jack."

"Is he your boyfriend?" Steven asked in a teasing voice.

"Steven," Elizabeth groaned. Steven is always teasing me and Elizabeth about boys. We don't want boyfriends, but that doesn't stop Steven. He likes to make us mad.

Molly didn't look mad at all. "Yes, he is," she said.

"Is he cute?" Steven said in that same awful tone of voice.

"Very," Molly said. "Do you have a pretty girlfriend?"

"No!" Steven said. His ears turned red.

I smiled at Molly. She really was

smart. Asking Steven about girls is a great way to shut him up.

"Did you make Jack a Valentine's Day card?" Elizabeth asked.

"No," Molly said. "I'm going to buy one."

"Maybe Jack will give you flowers," Elizabeth suggested.

Molly smiled. "That would be nice."

"Can we call Jack?" I asked.

"How come?" Molly asked.

"I want him to teach me how to juggle," I said. "I'm going to have a contest with a boy in my class. He keeps bragging about what a good juggler he is. I want to show him I'm better."

"That sounds important," Molly said.

"It is," I said. "Very."

"I'll ask your mom if it's OK to bring Jack over tomorrow," Molly said.

"Yippee!" I yelled. "I know Mom will say yes. Can't you call him right now?"

"Sorry," Molly said. "I have to talk to your mom first."

"OK," I agreed.

"Molly's nice," Elizabeth whispered to me.

I nodded. The new baby-sitter was nice. And best of all, she knew someone who could juggle.

CHAPTER 4

A Very Good Juggler

"Hi, I'm Jack."

"Hi!" I said.

"Hi!" Elizabeth said.

It was Wednesday. Elizabeth, Steven, and I had just gotten home from school. Molly and Jack were sitting on our front porch. They were holding hands.

Jack had black hair, bright blue eyes, and long legs. A blue backpack was sitting next to him.

Steven stared at Jack. "You're in middle school?" he asked.

I knew why Steven was surprised. Molly had told us she was in seventh grade. But Jack looked older.

"No, I'm not," Jack said. "I go to Sweet Valley High."

"Wow," Elizabeth whispered to me. "Molly is dating an older boy."

"She must be really popular," I whispered back.

"I saw Sweet Valley High's basketball team play last week," Steven told Jack. "I went to a game with my friend Joe. They won by twelve points."

"I was at that game," Jack said. "I'm on the team. I play forward."

"Wow," Steven breathed. "You must be a great player."

"Not that great," Jack said. "I sit on the bench a lot. It's only my first year of high school."

"I think you're great," Molly told

Jack. "When the coach lets you play, you score a lot of points."

Steven is a basketball freak. But I think basketball is boring. So does Elizabeth. Besides, Jack had come to our house to see me, not Steven.

"Will you please teach me how to juggle now?" I asked Jack.

Jack smiled. "You must be Jessica."

"Yes, I am," I replied. "And I really need to learn how to juggle."

"OK," Jack said. "I'll teach you right now." He unzipped his backpack and took out three brightly colored sacks. Then he stood up.

Elizabeth and I sat down next to Molly. Steven sat down, too. I was surprised. Steven never hangs out with us after school.

"What are you doing?" I whispered to Steven.

"I want to see Jack juggle," Steven said.

"These sacks are filled with sand," Jack said. He handed one to me.

"It's heavy," I said.

Jack nodded. "These are the best things to use when you're learning to juggle. They don't roll when you drop them."

"You mean *if* I drop them," I said.

Jack shook his head. "I mean *when*. You'll drop these a lot. Learning to juggle is hard. It takes a lot of practice."

I nodded. I had figured that out already.

"The first thing you need to learn is how to throw," Jack said. "Practice throwing one sack from your left hand to your right hand and back to your left hand. The sack should go up in an arc about as high as the top of your head. Once you learn to do that, I'll show you the next step."

"OK," I said. That sounded easy enough.

"I brought these sacks for you to borrow," Jack told me.

"Thanks," I said, taking them.

"Don't we get to see you juggle?" Molly asked Jack.

"Yeah!"

"Come on!"

"Please?"

"Sure," Jack said. He took the sacks back. A second later, they were flying through the air in a circle.

At first, Jack threw the sacks exactly as high as the top of his head. "This is the height you're aiming for," he reminded me.

I nodded.

"Show them something fancy," Molly suggested.

"OK," Jack said. He threw the sacks so that they soared way up into the air. Then he threw them only a few inches above his hands.

"Wow," Elizabeth breathed.

"That's good," I said.

Steven clapped.

"Thanks," Jack said. He caught the sacks and handed them back to me.

"Hey, Jack," Steven said. "Can you juggle basketballs?"

Molly laughed. "Jack can juggle anything."

"I want to see," Steven said. He ran to the garage. We had only one basketball. Steven brought out the basketball, Elizabeth's soccer ball, and my Frisbee. Jack juggled all three of them together.

Then Molly announced that it was time for our snack. We went inside for oatmeal cookies. While we ate, Jack juggled oranges.

"What else can you juggle?" I asked.

"Anything," Jack said.

Elizabeth looked around the kitchen. "How about plates?"

"Sure," Jack answered. "Plates, bowls, cups, you name it."

"Let's see," Steven said.

"No way," Molly said quickly. "I don't want any broken dishes."

"Don't worry," Steven said. "Jack never drops anything."

"He's an excellent juggler," I agreed.

"No dishes," Molly repeated.

Jack winked at us. "Molly's right. I do drop things sometimes."

After we finished our snack, we went back outside. I practiced throwing my sacks. Elizabeth, Steven, Jack, and Molly played tag until Mom came home.

"How's it going?" Mom called from the driveway.

"Great!" I told her. "I'm learning how to juggle."

"Good for you," Mom said.

"Hello, Mrs. Wakefield," Molly said.

"This is my friend Jack. I asked you if he could come over, remember?"

"I remember," Mom said. "Nice to meet you, Jack."

"Nice to meet you," Jack replied.

"You can take off now," Mom told Molly. "I'll take over."

"No," I moaned. I grabbed Jack's hand. "You can't leave. What about my juggling?"

"I'm sorry," Jack told me. "But I have to go to work."

"But *you* can stay," Elizabeth told Molly.

Molly shook her head. "I have homework to do. But I'll see you guys tomorrow."

"Will you come tomorrow, too?" I asked Jack.

"Jessica," Mom said, "Jack has other things to do."

Jack smiled. "I don't mind," he told

Mom. "Jessica has a big juggling contest coming up. I want her to be ready."

"Hurray!" I yelled.

"That's sweet of you," Mom told Jack.

"See you tomorrow," Jack and Molly called as they left.

I was so happy, I spun around in a circle. I would definitely beat Winston now.

CHAPTER 5

Molly's Broken Heart

I practiced all Wednesday evening. By bedtime, I had gotten pretty good at throwing one sack up at just the right height—and catching it.

On Thursday afternoon Jack came over, just as he had promised. He and Molly were sitting on our front porch when we got home from school.

Steven and Elizabeth were happy to see Jack and Molly. But they were bored with juggling. After we had our snack, Steven and Elizabeth went to the park to play. I had Jack and Molly to myself.

I showed Jack how well I could throw. "You can add another sack now," he said. I was happy. But not for long. That second sack made things much harder.

I had to start with both sacks in my left hand. Then I had to throw one into the air and count to two. Next, I was supposed to throw the other sack into the air and catch the first sack with my right hand. *Then* I had to catch the second one with my right hand.

After that, Jack had me practice throwing the sacks with my right hand and catching with my left.

I made lots of mistakes. But Jack didn't get mad at me. He sat on the porch with Molly and gave me advice.

I learned a few things about Molly and Jack that afternoon. When Jack was around, Molly got a silly look on her face. She giggled a lot. Jack liked to touch Molly's hand. Once he brushed her bangs off her face. I pretended not to notice. It was mushy.

After trying and trying, I finally threw both sacks and caught them just like Jack had shown me. "Did you see that?" I cried.

Nobody answered.

Jack and Molly weren't even watching me. Jack was whispering something in Molly's ear. She was looking down at her lap. Her face was bright red. I was mad. They had missed my great juggling. I stomped over to them.

"No fair secrets!" I yelled.

Molly looked up at me. "We're not telling secrets."

"Then what are you doing?" I asked.

"Making plans for Valentine's Day," Jack said.

"Oh," I said. "What are you going to do?"

"Something romantic," Jack said. He winked at Molly.

"Like what?" I asked.

"That's for us to know," Molly said.

That sounded like a secret to me!

"Are you going to practice your juggling again this afternoon?" Elizabeth asked me the next day. We were on the bus home.

"Yes," I said. "Jack is coming over to help me. I hope he'll come over on Saturday and Sunday, too."

Elizabeth groaned. "Aren't you ever going to get tired of juggling?"

"I'm already tired of it," I admitted.

"Then how come you're practicing so much?" Elizabeth asked.

"Because I want to beat Winston," I said.

Elizabeth nodded. "The juggling contest is on Tuesday. If you practice every

43

day until then, there's no way you can lose."

I nodded. I was sure I was going to win. "Jack is my secret weapon."

Elizabeth and I ran home from the bus stop. Steven had to stay late at school to work on a science project. When we got to our house, Molly and Jack weren't sitting on the porch.

"They must be inside," Elizabeth said.

We let ourselves into the house. Molly was in the kitchen. "Hi, Molly," I said. "Where's Jack?"

"I don't know," Molly said. "And I don't care."

Elizabeth put her books down on the table. "Your eyes are red," she told Molly.

Molly sniffled. "I've been crying."

"What's wrong?" I asked.

"Jack and I had a fight," Molly said.

"A big fight?" Elizabeth asked.

"Huge. We broke up." Molly blew her nose. "I can't believe it. We've been going together for five whole weeks."

Elizabeth and I traded worried looks.

Molly took a shaky breath. Tears welled up in her eyes.

Elizabeth put her arm around Molly's shoulders.

"Don't cry," I said.

Molly took a quick breath. "Don't worry," she said. "I'm fine. So, what do you two want for a snack?"

Elizabeth didn't answer. Neither did I. Who could think about food at a time like that?

Molly made herself smile. "I'm fine!" she said. "Really." But her voice was wobbly.

"What did you fight about?" Elizabeth asked.

Molly sighed. "You guys are too young to understand."

"No, we're not," I said.

"Well . . ." Molly said. "OK. I'll try to explain. Yesterday, I told Jack about a party my best friend is having. We talked about it for almost ten minutes." Molly's voice wasn't wobbly anymore. In fact, she was starting to sound angry. "Today I said something about the party to Jack. And he didn't even know what I was talking about!"

"How come?" I asked.

"Because he never listens to me!" Molly yelled.

"He doesn't?" I asked. I thought of how Jack and Molly had whispered about Valentine's Day. Hadn't he been listening to her then?

"No," Molly said. "Men are terrible listeners!"

"Maybe he just forgot about the party," Elizabeth suggested.

"After one day?" Molly asked.

Elizabeth shrugged. "Jessica is always forgetting her milk money. And Mom reminds her every day to take it."

"This is different," Molly said.

"I think you should tell Jack you're sorry," I told Molly.

"Me?" Molly said. "Why should I say I'm sorry?"

"Because you look sad," I explained. "You were happier when Jack was your boyfriend." That wasn't the *only* reason I wanted Molly to make up with Jack. After all, I needed Jack. I couldn't beat Winston without him.

"I do wish we'd make up," Molly said. "But Jack has to say he's sorry first!"

CHAPTER 6

Jack's Broken Heart

"Hi, Jessica," Elizabeth called on Saturday morning. She was skipping across our lawn toward me.

Elizabeth was in her bathing suit, and she had a towel wrapped around her shoulders. She had been swimming in our pool with Steven and Dad. I love to swim. But I hadn't been in the pool that morning—I had been practicing my juggling since just after breakfast.

"How's it going?" Elizabeth asked.

I caught one of my sacks. "Terrible!" I said. My other sack was lying on the ground. I bent down to pick it up. "I keep making the same mistake. But I'm not sure why."

"Jack could tell you," Elizabeth said.

I sighed. "I know. I wish he were here."

Mom poked her head out the back door. "Daddy and I have to run some errands at the mall," she called. "We're going to eat lunch there. Come inside and get ready."

"All right!" Elizabeth said with a grin. She started toward the house.

I ran after Elizabeth. I love the mall. Besides, I was ready to take a break. I was tired of juggling. It would have been fun if I had been getting better. But my juggling hadn't improved since my last lesson with Jack.

A few minutes later, we were sitting in the food court at the mall. Mom and

Dad were eating salads. Elizabeth and I each had a slice of pizza. Steven had two slices.

Steven's friend Joe came over. He asked Steven to go to the arcade and play video games.

"Who wants ice cream?" Dad asked after Steven ran off with Joe.

"Me!"

"Me!"

Mom smiled. "Let's go."

On the way to the ice cream store, we went window shopping. That's when you look at what is in the stores' windows without going inside.

The toy store's window was full of windup toys. They were jumping and rolling all over each other.

Fuzzy brown puppies were playing in the pet store window.

In the camera shop, a big machine was printing photographs.

"This is an excellent day for window shopping," Elizabeth said.

I agreed. There were lots of exciting things to see. But the most exciting thing of all was inside the ice cream store.

"Jack!" I yelled as we walked inside. He was standing behind the counter, wearing an apron.

Elizabeth and I ran up to him.

"Hi, you guys," Jack said. "How's the juggling going?"

"Not good," I said. "I need more lessons."

"Sorry," Jack said. "I won't be able to give you any more."

"Please?" I said. "Pretty, pretty please?"

"The juggling contest is really soon," Elizabeth added.

"I'm sorry," Jack repeated. He sounded like he wasn't going to change his mind.

"Molly told us you had a fight," Elizabeth said.

"We did," Jack said, looking sad. "That's why I can't give Jessica lessons. I don't want to see Molly at your house."

"If you came over, maybe you would make up," I said.

"I wish we would make up," Jack said. "But Molly has to say she's sorry first. So . . . What would you like to eat?"

Jack made our ice cream cones. He even put sprinkles on them. That made me feel a tiny bit better. But I still wanted to beat Winston. And without Jack, I knew I probably wouldn't.

CHAPTER 7

My Great Idea

"**D**on't go away, kids! The show will continue after these messages. . . ." A commercial came on the television.

"I'm bored," Elizabeth said with a giant yawn. "Let's go upstairs and get some toys."

Elizabeth was still dressed in her pajamas. So was I. It was Sunday morning. We wanted to play outside, but it was raining.

"I don't want to miss the show," I said.

"If we hurry, we'll get back before the commercials are over," Elizabeth said.

I sighed. "You go."

"OK," Elizabeth said. "Do you want me to bring down your juggling stuff?"

"No," I said.

"But you haven't practiced since yesterday morning," Elizabeth said. "The juggling contest is the day after tomorrow."

I shrugged. "I'm never going to beat Winston now. Jack didn't even teach me how to juggle with all three sacks."

"Don't give up," Elizabeth said.

I didn't answer. I just stared at the TV.

"Geez," Elizabeth mumbled. "What a grump." She went upstairs alone.

Elizabeth was right. I was grumpy. The TV was making it worse. It was the day before Valentine's Day. All the commercials were for sappy lovey-dovey stuff. It was enough to make me sick. Also, I was unhappy about the juggling contest. I didn't want to lose. But to beat Winston, I needed Jack. I wished he and Molly would make up.

"Flowers," said the TV announcer. "They say all the things you'd like to say—but can't."

Maybe Molly should buy some flowers, I thought. *They could tell Jack she was sorry. . . .*

Of course, I knew that was silly. Flowers can't talk. Only people can talk. That's when I got an idea!

Molly wouldn't say she was sorry. Jack wouldn't say he was sorry. But *I* would.

CHAPTER 8

Love Letters

I jumped up, turned off the TV, and ran upstairs.

"Where are you going?" Elizabeth asked. She was coming down the stairs with an armful of toys.

"To our room," I said. "Come on. I have a great idea."

"What is it?" Elizabeth asked.

"Do you want Molly and Jack to get back together?" I said.

"Sure," Elizabeth said.

"Well, I know how to do it," I told her. "We have to write Jack a letter."

Elizabeth followed me up to our room.

"The letter has to look like it's from Molly," I went on. "Your handwriting is more grown-up than mine. You write it."

Elizabeth shook her head. "I don't understand. If the letter is from Molly, why are we writing it?"

"I said it has to *look* like it's from Molly," I explained. "Just get a piece of paper. I'll tell you what to write."

Elizabeth got the paper and sat down at her desk. I told Elizabeth what to say. When I finished, Elizabeth studied what she had written. "It's not quite right," she said. "I think it should be more mushy."

I groaned. But I let Elizabeth put in some mushy parts. She's the writer, not me.

"Perfect!" Elizabeth announced a

few minutes later. She copied the whole thing onto a piece of our special pink stationery. This is what the letter said:

Dear Jack,

I am very, very sorry about our fight. I can't live without you. Please meet me in the park at 3:30 on Valentine's Day. I'll be under the big tree.

Love and kisses,
Molly

"I like it," I said. "Now write one from Jack to Molly."

Elizabeth chewed on her pencil. "I don't think I should."

"Why not?" I asked.

"Because my handwriting doesn't look like a boy's," Elizabeth explained.

"Let's get Steven," I suggested.

Elizabeth and I ran to Steven's room. We knocked.

"Go away!" Steven yelled.

Elizabeth rolled her eyes at me.

"We're coming in on three!" I yelled. "One, two, three!" I pushed open Steven's door.

Steven was lying on his bed, reading a comic book. He pretended not to notice us when we walked in.

"Steven, we need your help," Elizabeth said.

"We're doing something nice for Molly and Jack," I added.

That got Steven's attention. "Like what?" he asked.

"Like getting them back together," I said.

"How do you know they want to get back together?" Steven asked. "Maybe they like being broken up. Maybe Jack wants more time to play basketball."

"But they're in love!" I said.

Elizabeth and Steven both rolled their eyes.

I giggled. "They want to make up. They just don't know how to say they're sorry."

Still, Steven wouldn't agree to help us until we promised to set the table on his night for a week. Then he got out a piece of lined notebook paper. He copied the letter Elizabeth and I had written, only his letter was addressed to Molly and signed with Jack's name.

"Everything's set," I said as Steven handed me the letter.

"Not really," Elizabeth said. "We still have to get the letters to Jack and Molly."

I smiled. "Leave that to me."

CHAPTER 9

Back to the Mall

"**D**addy?" I said.

It was that same day. We had just finished dinner. Mom and Dad were clearing the table. Steven had gone outside to play. It was the perfect time for Elizabeth and me to put part two of our plan into action.

"What is it, honey?" Dad asked.

"The ice cream we had yesterday was really good," I said.

"I'm glad you enjoyed it," Dad said. He handed a stack of dirty dishes to Mom. She started to rinse them and put them into the dishwasher.

"I liked it, too," Elizabeth put in.

"And so did you," I reminded Dad. "You said your hot fudge sundae was yummy."

"Mm-hmm," Dad said. He wasn't paying much attention to me. He was busy wiping off the table.

"I was thinking," I went on. "It's too bad Steven didn't get to go to the ice cream store with us."

Mom turned away from the sink and gave me a surprised look. I'm usually not worried about Steven. Uh-oh! Mom was going to see through our plan. I glanced at Elizabeth. What should I do now?

"See, Steven has been kind of sad lately," Elizabeth said quickly. "He really misses Jack."

"He doesn't seem sad to me," Mom said. "He ate three hot dogs for dinner."

"He's sad *and* hungry," Elizabeth agreed.

"That's why we want to go to the ice cream store," I put in. "So Steven can see Jack. And eat ice cream."

"But we already had dessert," Mom said.

"Just fruit salad," I said. "That's not really dessert. It's good for you."

"That sundae *was* yummy," Dad said helpfully.

"So, can we go?" Elizabeth asked.

"I guess," Mom said.

"I'll get Steven," I said.

A few minutes later, Dad was parking at the mall.

"What if Jack isn't working?" Elizabeth whispered to me as we climbed out of the van.

"I didn't think of that," I whispered back.

Elizabeth thought for a second.

"Don't worry," she said. "He has to be working."

I nodded. I chewed on my thumbnail as we walked through the mall. If Jack *wasn't* working, my plan would be destroyed. I let out a big sigh of relief when we got to the ice cream store. I was lucky. Jack was working.

"Hi, Jessica and Elizabeth," he greeted us. "You must really like ice cream. Hey, Steven! How's your foul shot coming?"

I waited while Jack and Steven talked about basketball.

I waited while everyone ordered. I asked for a chocolate cone. Elizabeth wanted a strawberry cone. Dad said he would have another hot fudge sundae.

I waited while Jack got us our ice cream.

Then, finally, I gave Jack the note.

"Molly wants you to have this," I whispered.

"OK, kids," Dad called. "Let's move out."

"Bye, Jack," we all yelled.

"Bye," he yelled back. He was reading the note. He was smiling.

Out in the mall, Elizabeth gave me a hug.

"One down," I said.

"One to go," Elizabeth added.

CHAPTER 10

Happy Valentine's Day!

"Happy Valentine's Day," Mrs. Otis said.

"Happy Valentine's Day," Elizabeth and I both answered.

It was the next afternoon. Our class was having its Valentine's Day party. We were drinking cherry punch and eating heart-shaped candy.

"Here are your valentines," Mrs. Otis said. She handed a big bunch of cards to Elizabeth. They were held together by a rubber band. She gave another bunch to me.

Mrs. Otis has a rule. Everyone in our class has to give a valentine to everyone else. I don't like the rule. I didn't want to give a card to Winston.

Elizabeth thinks it's a good rule. She doesn't like anyone to have their feelings hurt.

"Ooh," Lila said. Her desk is next to mine. "The valentine you gave me is cool!"

"Thanks," I said. I had given Lila one of the best cards I made. I had used lots of silver and gold and copper crayon. It looked extra special.

I ripped open the card on the top of my pile. "It's from Winston," I told Elizabeth and Lila. I held the card up. They leaned over to see.

The card said, "To the second-best juggler in Mrs. Otis's class. From the very, very *bestest!*"

"Winston makes me so mad," I said.

Elizabeth laughed. "He wants to win the juggling contest as much as you do."

"That's too bad," I said. "Because he's not going to win."

"Have you been practicing?" Lila asked.

"Lots," I told her.

"Are you ready?" Lila asked.

"Well . . ." I still didn't know how to juggle all three sacks. "Almost."

"You don't have much more time to practice," Lila said. "The juggling contest is tomorrow."

I could feel my face getting red. "I'll be ready. Don't worry."

Lila shrugged. She went back to opening her cards.

I leaned toward Elizabeth. "Everything has to go perfectly this afternoon."

"I know," Elizabeth said. "I'm ready."

Later, on our front porch, Elizabeth pulled the note for Molly out of her spelling book. Steven was still at school. He had to work on his science project again.

"Are you sure you know what to do?" I whispered.

"Yes," Elizabeth whispered.

We each took a deep breath.

"One, two, three!" I whispered.

Elizabeth opened the front door.

"Molly, where are you?" I yelled as we rushed inside. "Look what we found!"

"Here I am," Molly called. "What did you find?"

"This!" Elizabeth held out the letter. "It has your name on it."

"It was taped to the front door," I added.

"Really?" Molly said. "It wasn't there when I came in."

"Someone must have just put it there," I said.

"Read it," Elizabeth told Molly.

Molly opened the letter. She read it. She smiled. "Go get ready," she said.

"Get ready?" I asked innocently. "Where are we going?"

"To the park," Molly said.

"Aren't we going to have a snack first?" Elizabeth asked.

"Nope," Molly said. "There's no time." About two seconds later, Molly rushed us out the door.

"I'm hungry," Elizabeth whispered to me.

"Me too," I said. "But this is going to be worth it."

CHAPTER 11

Smooches

"What time is it?" I asked Molly. Elizabeth, Molly, and I were sitting under the big tree in the park.

"It's 3:31," Molly said.

Elizabeth and I traded looks. In the note, we had told Jack to meet Molly at three thirty. He was late. I was worried. But I had to pretend I wasn't. Molly wasn't supposed to know that Elizabeth and I knew we were waiting for Jack.

I lay back in the grass. Above me, the tree branches swayed back and forth. I studied them for a long time. Then I rolled over on my side and watched Elizabeth. She was trying to make a necklace out of clover.

"Molly?" I asked. "What time is it?"

"It's 3:33," Molly answered. "Two minutes since the last time you asked."

"Oh," I said.

"Why don't you guys go play?" Molly suggested. "I bet some of your friends are here."

"No," I said.

"No, thanks," Elizabeth said.

I wanted to be with Molly when Jack arrived—*if* Jack arrived. Elizabeth must have felt the same way.

I wondered what would happen. Would Jack and Molly make up? Would they fight more? Would they discover that we had written the notes? Maybe Jack wanted to come to the park, but couldn't. What if he had to work?

Waiting was hard. But then, just when I was about to give up, I saw him! Jack was hurrying toward the big tree. He was carrying a bunch of flowers and a box of candy.

Molly saw him, too. She stood up.

I nudged Elizabeth. We stood up, too.

Jack rushed up to us. "Molly, I'm so—"

"Shh." Molly put a finger over Jack's lips. She stepped very, very close to him. Jack and Molly kissed. On the lips.

"Eww," Elizabeth said.

I covered my eyes. "Gross!"

Molly and Jack kept kissing.

Elizabeth made a face. I held my nose.

Molly and Jack kept kissing.

I pulled on Molly's sleeve. She and Jack looked down at me. "Cut it out!" I said.

Molly laughed. "Sorry."

Jack held the chocolate and flowers out to Molly. The flowers were a little smashed. "These are for you," he said.

"Thanks," Molly said. "Would anyone like a piece of chocolate?"

"Yes!" I said.

"Yes, please," Elizabeth said.

Molly opened the box and held it out. Elizabeth and I helped ourselves. Yummy. I love chocolate.

"Do you have your juggling sacks with you?" Jack asked me.

"No," I mumbled with my mouth full. "They're at home."

"Well, then, let's go," Jack said.

Molly and Jack held hands and whispered all the way back to our house. Elizabeth and I skipped after them.

"Hey, you guys," Elizabeth said. "Are you going out for Valentine's Day?"

"Sure," Jack said. "We're going to go to a movie."

"And then get some ice cream," Molly added.

"At the ice cream store?" I asked.

"Where else?" Jack said.

When we got back to the house, Jack gave me a juggling lesson. He showed me how to juggle with all three sacks. I felt great. I was positive I would beat Winston the next day.

CHAPTER 12

Juggling

"Are you ready?" I asked Winston during recess the next day.

Winston nodded. "Ready."

Most of Mrs. Otis's class was gathered on the playground. It was time for the juggling contest!

"How will we know who wins?" Kisho asked.

"I guess we need a judge," Winston said.

"OK," I said. "I'll pick. I want Lila to be the judge."

"No fair," Winston said. "Lila will

say you were better no matter what."

"Then you pick a judge, too," I suggested.

"OK," Winston said. "I pick Todd."

"Wait," Todd said. "What if Lila votes for one of you, and I pick the other? It would be a tie. We need one more judge."

"Right," Amy said. "Someone Jessica and Winston both trust to be fair."

"Elizabeth," Winston and I said together.

You might think it's funny that Winston chose my twin sister. But everyone knows Elizabeth is trustworthy.

Lila, Todd, and Elizabeth came to the front of the crowd.

"Who's going to go first?" Elizabeth asked.

"Me," Winston said.

I shrugged. "Fine."

Winston stepped forward and started to juggle three tennis balls.

"He's good," Ellen whispered to me.

I wrinkled my nose. Winston *was* good at keeping the balls in the air. But watching him juggle wasn't much fun—he wasn't paying attention to his audience. His eyes were on the tennis balls. I usually focused on my sacks, too. But watching Winston gave me a great idea. I was going to put a little more pizzazz in my act.

After Winston finished, he took a deep bow. Everyone clapped for him. Winston smirked at me. I could tell he thought he had done really well.

I stepped forward. I gave everyone a dazzling smile. I started to juggle my sacks. As soon as I got them going, I looked at the crowd and smiled again. Almost everyone smiled back. *I'm definitely going to win,* I thought.

I glanced back up at my sacks. One of them was falling too far to the right. I leaned over to catch it. At the same time, I had to throw another sack into the air. I threw it much too hard. The sack flew out into the crowd of kids.

"Ouch!" Amy yelled.

I turned to see what had happened. My sack had hit Amy in the head! "Oops," I said.

"Are you all right?"

"That *had* to hurt!"

Everyone was talking at once.

"I'm fine," Amy said.

I glanced back up at my other two sacks. But they weren't in the air anymore. They were on the ground. I had missed them while I was looking at Amy. I quickly picked those two sacks up.

"Amy, throw me my sack," I called. "I'm going to go again."

"No way," Winston yelled. "I only went once."

"But I messed up," I shouted. "I get another turn."

"That's not fair," Winston yelled.

"Is so!" I shouted.

Todd stepped between us. "Let the judges decide."

The judges said I couldn't go again. Then they said Winston had won. Two votes to one!

"I can't believe you voted for Winston," I told Elizabeth as we walked home from the bus stop.

Elizabeth giggled. "Come on, Jessica. You hit Amy in the head!"

"I still think I should have won," I said. "I'm a better juggler than Winston. Jack was a really good teacher. And I practiced a lot."

"I know," Elizabeth said. "You probably would have won if you hadn't tried to show off."

My jaw dropped. "I wasn't showing off!"

"Jessica—" Elizabeth said.

"OK," I admitted. "I was showing off a little." I was upset. I hate to lose.

"Well, at least we helped Jack and Molly," Elizabeth said.

"That's the important thing, right?"

"I guess. . . ." I said.

We walked up our front walk and let ourselves into the house.

Molly was doing her homework in the kitchen. She closed her history book when she saw us. "How are my little matchmakers?" Molly asked.

"Fine," Elizabeth said.

"What did you call us?" I asked.

"Oops," Molly said. "Well, I guess I can tell you the truth now. Jack and I knew you guys wrote the notes."

"We didn't fool you?" I asked.

"No," Molly said.

"Then why did you go to the park?" Elizabeth asked.

Molly smiled a silly smile. "Love," she said.

"Love?" Elizabeth repeated.

I stuck out my tongue. Who needed love? Boys are yucky. Even Elizabeth thinks so sometimes.

Molly laughed. "You'll understand someday."

I didn't tell Molly, but she was one hundred percent wrong. I, Jessica Wakefield, will never like boys.

Will Jessica and Elizabeth learn to like boys? Find out in Sweet Valley Kids #57, NO GIRLS ALLOWED.

SIGN UP FOR THE SWEET VALLEY HIGH® FAN CLUB!

Hey, girls! Get all the gossip on Sweet Valley High's® most popular teenagers when you join our fantastic Fan Club! As a member, you'll get all of this really cool stuff:

- Membership Card with your own personal Fan Club ID number
- A Sweet Valley High® Secret Treasure Box
- Sweet Valley High® Stationery
- Official Fan Club Pencil (for secret note writing!)
- Three Bookmarks
- A "Members Only" Door Hanger
- Two Skeins of J. & P. Coats® Embroidery Floss with flower barrette instruction leaflet
- Two editions of *The Oracle* newsletter
- Plus exclusive Sweet Valley High® product offers, special savings, contests, and much more!

Be the first to find out what Jessica & Elizabeth Wakefield are up to by joining the Sweet Valley High® Fan Club for the one-year membership fee of only $6.25 each for U.S. residents, $8.25 for Canadian residents (U.S. currency). Includes shipping & handling.

Send a check or money order (do not send cash) made payable to "Sweet Valley High® Fan Club" along with this form to:

SWEET VALLEY HIGH® FAN CLUB, BOX 3919-B, SCHAUMBURG, IL 60168-3919

NAME _____
                        (Please print clearly)

ADDRESS _____

CITY_____ STATE _____ ZIP_____
                                                        (Required)

AGE _____ BIRTHDAY_____ /_____ /_____

Offer good while supplies last. Allow 6-8 weeks after check clearance for delivery. Addresses without ZIP codes cannot be honored. Offer good in USA & Canada only. Void where prohibited by law.
©1993 by Francine Pascal   LCI-1383-123